A Note to Parents and Caregivers:

Read-it! Readers are for children who are just starting on the amazing road to reading. These beautiful books support both the acquisition of reading skills and the love of books.

The PURPLE LEVEL presents basic topics and objects using high frequency words and simple language patterns.

The RED LEVEL presents familiar topics using common words and repeating sentence patterns.

The BLUE LEVEL presents new ideas using a larger vocabulary and varied sentence structure.

The YELLOW LEVEL presents more challenging ideas, a broad vocabulary, and wide variety in sentence structure.

The GREEN LEVEL presents more complex ideas, an extended vocabulary range, and expanded language structures.

The ORANGE LEVEL presents a wide range of ideas and concepts using challenging vocabulary and complex language structures.

When sharing a book with your child, read in short stretches, pausing often to talk about the pictures. Have your child turn the pages and point to the pictures and familiar words. And be sure to reread favorite stories or parts of stories.

There is no right or wrong way to share books with children. Find time to read with your child, and pass on the legacy of literacy.

Adria F. Klein, Ph.D.
Professor Emeritus
California State University
San Bernardino, California

Editors: Christianne Jones and Dodie Marie Miller
Page Production: Brandie Shoemaker
Art Director: Nathan Gassman

First American edition published in 2007 by
Picture Window Books
5115 Excelsior Boulevard
Suite 232
Minneapolis, MN 55416
877-845-8392
www.picturewindowbooks.com

This Americanization of TROMSO THE TROLL was originally published in
English in 2003 under the title SNOW TROLL by arrangement with Oxford
University Press.

Printed in the United States of America.

Library of Congress Cataloging-in-Publication Data
McAllister, Margaret (Margaret I.)
Tromso the troll / by Margaret McAllister ; illustrated by Steve Cox.
p. cm. — (Read-it! readers)
Summary: Happy to be invited to his friend Peter's birthday party, Tromso the troll
decides to make him a very special "cake."
ISBN-13: 978-1-4048-3144-5 (library binding)
ISBN-10: 1-4048-3144-4 (library binding)
[1. Trolls—Fiction. 2. Birthdays—Fiction. 3. Parties—Fiction. 4. Friendship—
Fiction.] I. Cox, Steve, 1961- ill. II. Title.
PZ7.M4782525Tro 2006
[E]—dc22   2006029127

Tromso the Troll

by Margaret McAllister
illustrated by Steve Cox

Special thanks to our advisers for their expertise:

Adria F. Klein, Ph.D.
Professor Emeritus, California State University
San Bernardino, California

Susan Kesselring, M.A.
Literacy Educator
Rosemount–Apple Valley–Eagan (Minnesota) School District

PICTURE WINDOW BOOKS
Minneapolis, Minnesota

Tromso was a tame troll. He lived in a village called Hoppings. It was at the bottom of a mountain.

Everybody liked Tromso. He was very helpful. If anybody asked, he would cut down a tree or build a wall.

5

To thank him for his help, people gave him things. What he liked most were cakes, bananas, bricks, cabbages, old chair legs, and jigsaw puzzles with pieces missing.

Tromso kept everything. He used the things to fix his house. And if he was hungry, he ate them.

Peter and Joy were Tromso's friends. One morning, Tromso was at their house when the mail carrier came. Tromso saw pieces of paper drop through the mail slot.

"What are those?" asked Tromso.

"Letters," said Peter.

Tromso wanted to get letters, too. When he went home, he made a mail slot in his front door.

All the next day and the day after that, Tromso stayed home. Peter went to see him.

When Peter arrived at Tromso's house, Tromso was sitting sadly on the floor, eating a brick.

"My mail slot doesn't work," said Tromso. "I made a mail slot to get letters, but they don't ever come."

"Poor Tromso!" said Peter. "Somebody has to send you the letters!"

"Oh," said Tromso. "I hope somebody sends me some soon."

The next morning, a blue envelope fell through Tromso's mail slot. The envelope had a birthday cake on the front and was addressed to Tromso.

Tromso the Troll
417 Appleton Lane
Hoppings

Tromso was excited. He opened the envelope and read the note inside.

Dear Tromso,

You are invited to my birthday party at 3 o'clock on Saturday. See you there!

From,
Peter

Tromso ran over to Peter and Joy's house.
"I got your invitation!" he said.

"Good!" said Peter. "Have you read it?"

"I did," Tromso said, "but I don't understand. I know Sunday and Monday are days of the week, but what is a 'birthday'?"

Peter told him about birthdays and parties. He also told him about birthday cakes.

"My mom always makes a big cake for my birthday," said Peter.

"How does she make the birthday cake?" asked Tromso.

"She mixes up lots of nice things," said Peter. "Then she puts decorations and candles on top."

That gave Tromso an idea for the perfect birthday present for Peter. Tromso ran home to get started.

Tromso looked in his junk heap for things he liked to eat. He found pebbles, old chairs, string, and sand. He stirred them up with plenty of glue. Then he put everything in the sun to dry. He couldn't wait to give Peter his present.

On Peter's birthday, everyone gave him presents. Tromso was saving his present for later.

After gifts, everyone played games. They played Blind Man's Bluff. Tromso fell in the duck pond.

They played Pass the Present. Tromso ate the
wrapping paper.

They played hide-and-seek. Tromso was too
big to hide anywhere.

Then Peter and Joy passed out the birthday cake. It was time for Tromso to give Peter his gift.

"Surprise!" said Tromso as he showed everyone the cake he had made.

"It looks very nice," said Peter. But it didn't. Nobody wanted to eat it. Then Peter had an idea.

"That cake is too special to eat," he said.

"We'll keep it outside," said Joy. "We could play on it."

"It's a very strong cake," said Tromso. "It won't break if you climb on it."

So they put the cake beside the duck pond for everyone to play on. The children loved Tromso's gift to Peter.

Tromso was happy to have such good friends.
He had a great time at his first birthday party.

More *Read-it!* Readers

Bright pictures and fun stories help you practice your reading skills. Look for more books at your level.

Alex and Toolie

Another Pet

The Big Pig

Bliss, Blueberries, and the Butterfly

Camden's Game

Cass the Monkey

Charlie's Tasks

Clever Cat

Flora McQuack

Kyle's Recess

Marconi the Wizard

Peppy, Patch, and the Postman

Peter's Secret

Pets on Vacation

The Princess and the Tower

Theodore the Millipede

The Three Princesses

Willie the Whale

The Zoo Band

Looking for a specific title or level? A complete list of *Read-it!* Readers is available on our Web site:

www.picturewindowbooks.com